THE STORY OF
LITTLE BLUE HOUND

A CRYSTAL TALE

WRITTEN BY ROGER NEAL   ILLUSTRATED BY STEVE BEEBE

THE STORY OF LITTLE BLUE HOUND
A Crystal Tale

By Roger Neal
Illustrated by Steve Beebe

Library of Congress Catalog Card Number
95-070508

International Standard Book Number
1-55605-261-8

Printed in the United States of America

Cloverdale Books for Children
Wyndham Hall Press
Bristol, IN   46507-9460

THE STORY OF LITTLE BLUE HOUND

(A Crystal Tale)

This story takes place in the high mountains of Crystal, Colorado in the late 1800s. On this day, the sheepherder and his dog, Little Blue Hound, had come down to the silver mining town of Crystal to buy supplies. The sheepherder told Little Blue Hound to STAY, while he was in the store.

After a short time, Little Blue Hound decided to take a walk down the street. Now, you have to remember that Blue was just a little dog and he didn't know any better than to walk down the middle of the street. And he certainly didn't know that the noon stage was going to be on time for the first time ever.

The people could hear the driver, winding down Sheep Mountain, yelling in a wild voice at his team of horses. The people were excited because this was the first time Charlie had ever been on time. "Come on Rubber Legs! Let's go Paint! We're going to be on time today!" hollered Charlie.

But Little Blue Hound didn't know the stage was coming. He saw the people standing on the sides of the dirt street, yelling and laughing, and he thought they were talking about him. So he just held his head high and kept walking down the middle of the street, right past the Delivery Station.

The sheepherder saw his dog and knew he had to get Little Blue Hound out of the road. But when he yelled, his voice just blended in with all of the other town's folk. The stage was getting closer and closer to Little Blue Hound and the sheepherder knew he was going to have to save his dog. The sheepherder ran out into the street and dove down on Little Blue Hound! Now they were both lying in the path of the rushing stage.

Charlie pulled back on the reins, "Whoa boys! Whoa! Whoa!" shouted Charlie. The horses came to a stop, with their hooves just short of the sheepherder, who was lying over Little Blue Hound. Everyone was upset with Little Blue Hound, because now the stage was late getting to the Delivery Station again. The sheepherder picked up Little Blue Hound and scolded him. Poor Little Blue Hound, he didn't understand. He was just a little dog.

The sheepherder loaded up his supplies and headed back up to the high country, where he had left the sheep dogs in charge of the sheep. Poor Little Blue Hound followed with his tail between his legs.

When they arrived at the camp, the sheepherder called his dogs in and fed them. Then he yelled at the dogs, "Hounds, go fetch the sheep!" At that, the dogs ran to bring the sheep down from the meadow. They knew it was time to bring the sheep back to camp before the sun went down. Little Blue Hound wanted to help but the sheepherder said, "No Little Blue Hound, you stay here. You're too little to help!"

As the dogs brought the sheep in, the sheepherder counted them, "One, two, three, four............two hundred one, two hundred two. Well, dogs, we're missing three sheep. Come on boys, let's see where they went!" The sheepherder knew it would soon be getting dark, so he got his rifle and a lantern. Then he mounted his horse. He told Little Blue Hound to STAY!

The sheepherder followed his dogs and soon they found some bloody wool and huge BEAR tracks leading up the back side of Devil's Ridge. "Come on dogs, let's fetch that bear," said the sheepherder, and the dogs went hounding up the steep mountain. Near the top of Devil's Ridge, the dogs stopped at an old mine and stood outside the entrance hounding and jumping up and down.

When the sheepherder arrived, he knew the bear must be in the mine.

The sheepherder dismounted and loaded three bullets into his big rifle. "O.K. hounds, I'm ready! Now go fetch that bear out of that mine and when he comes out, I'm going to shoot him dead!"

The hounds went down into the mine, with their hounding echoing back to the sheepherder, "HOUND, HOUND, HOUND HOUND!" Soon there was a tremendous, GROWL, and the hounds came running out, whimpering, with their tails between their legs. Disgusted, the sheepherder lit his lantern, picked up his rifle and said, "Well I guess I'll have to do this job by myself."

Slowly the sheepherder walked back into the mine, holding the lantern high in his left hand and the rifle in his right. Soon he could see the end of the mine. "Why, there's nothing down here but a big brown rock!" Just then, the big brown rock stood up. It was the biggest bear the sheepherder had ever seen. Holding the rifle with one hand was difficult, but the sheepherder knew he needed the light from the lantern. He raised the rifle to his shoulder and began to take careful aim. Just then he felt something clawing on his boot.

He looked down and saw Little Blue Hound. "LITTLE BLUE HOUND. GET OUT OF HERE!" But Little Blue Hound didn't understand. He put his head down and began walking TOWARD the bear. The sheepherder knew he had to act fast. Without taking aim, he raised his rifle and fired his first shot. The bullet went crashing into the rocks ricocheting past the bear. The bear knew he could be killed by the sheepherder's rifle and that the little dog could not hurt him. He let out another thundering GROWL and swiped at the air with both paws.

Meanwhile, the sheepherder reloaded his gun. "Come back Little Blue Hound," the sheepherder pleaded. But Little Blue Hound kept walking toward the bear. The sheepherder tried to raise his gun and take aim, but when he pulled the trigger, once again he was off the mark and the bullet just bounced off of the rocks.

Now the bear was getting tired and came down on all four paws. Little Blue Hound went walking past the bear. The bear took a swipe at Little Blue Hound, but the little dog thought this was just another big dog picking on him. As Blue walked behind the bear, the bear paid him no mind because he was still worried about the sheepherder and his rifle.

While the sheepherder reloaded the last bullet, Little Blue Hound was now behind the bear. He was tired from the long walk up Devil's Ridge and the nice soft fur on the bear's back looked like a nice place to lie down. So Little Blue Hound jumped up on the bear's back and started scratching out a place to lie down. Well, the bear didn't like that at all! He started to raise up and at the same moment the sheepherder fired his last bullet. He missed again, but rocks started to fall.

When one of the rocks hit Little Blue Hound, he knew he was in the wrong place. He jumped off of the bears back and started to run to the sheepherder. The bear sensed that the sheepherder was out of bullets and he rose up on his hind legs. As Little Blue Hound ran by, the bear knew he could get rid of this little pest once and for all. Just then, a gigantic rock fell, hitting the bear on top of his head. The bear fell forward, his massive weight falling right on poor Little Blue Hound. Poor Little Blue Hound was surely dead.

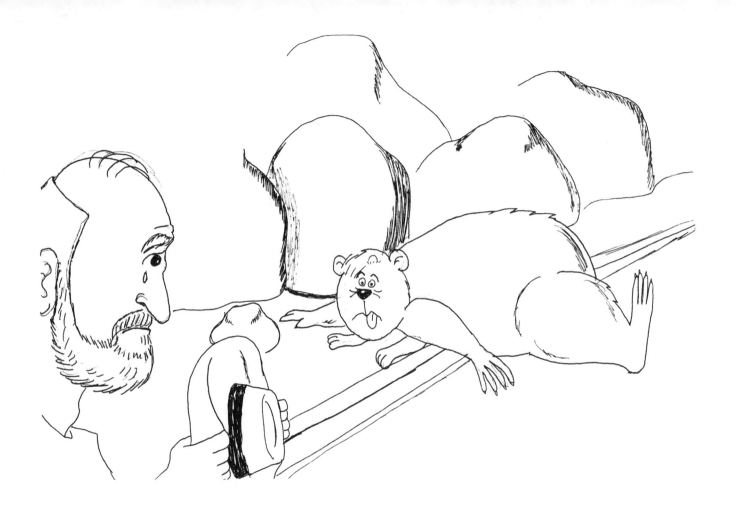

The sheepherder ran over to the bear and saw one of Little Blue Hound's paws sticking out from under the bear. The sheepherder began to cry, "Poor Little Blue Hound. You were the only dog that was brave enough to come in here with me. You weren't afraid of this bear. You just wanted to stay with me, and now you're dead. Good-bye Little Blue Hound. I'll never forget you." At that, the sheepherder wiped away his tears, picked up his lantern and gun and headed back home.

But wait! He heard a noise coming from the bear. He turned with his empty rifle. Out from underneath that nice soft fur came Little Blue Hound! He wasn't dead after all. He was just taking a nap under that nice soft fur. "Little Blue Hound! Come here boy! Tomorrow we are going to skin this bear and take the hide to town. We're going to show everybody what a brave dog can do."

Well, they did just that and then they had a big parade celebrating Little

Blue Hound. This time they WANTED Little Blue Hound to walk down the

center of Crystal and they all cheered the dog known as LITTLE BLUE

HOUND.

Today Crystal, Colorado is just a ghost town. But every summer, the old timers gather to listen once more to the story of Little Blue Hound.